Mr. Awesome Great Day

Mr. Awesome Great Day

Written by Rachelle Valenzuela

Illustrated by Sophia Trigonis

. to the dreamers, the thinkers,
ı little more faith over those
ıngly great fears.

On Arthur's very first day of first grade, he was given a homework assignment.
"Your assignment is to go home and write down what you want to
be when you grow up!" Arthur's teacher stated.

Arthur looked towards the ceiling with a puzzled but tiny smirk on his face. "I get to pick who I want to be when I grow up?" exclaimed Arthur. "How cool!"

Arthur shoved his papers into his backpack, scurried out of his seat, and rushed out the door.

Arthur zoomed through the front door and dashed into the kitchen, where he quickly greeted his mom and dad. "Hello! I have my very first homework paper thing!" exclaimed Arthur, "And I get to pick who I want to be when I grow up!" Arthur ran to his room before his parents could stop and give him his afternoon snack.

Arthur closed his door, hopped onto his chair, and scooted towards his desk. He began frantically writing ideas onto his paper. He pondered and thought about all the possibilities of who he could be one day. With a bright gleaming smile, Arthur grabbed his pencil and circled his new found idea. He could not wait to show his parents as he once again scurried off the edge of his seat.

"Mom, Dad, look! I know who I want to be when I grow up!" Arthur said excitedly as he jumped up and down. His mother reached down to see his paper and stared at it with confusion.

"Mr. Awesome Great Day?" asked his mom.

"Yeah!" exclaimed Arthur. "I'm going to tell everyone, 'Have a great day!' and they'll think I'm AWESOME!"

Arthur started to soar around the kitchen and made wooshing sounds with his cape. Arthur's dad chuckled to himself while he poured himself a cup of coffee. "That's not a real job though, sport. I think they are looking for something along the lines of a doctor...or lawyer. Don't you want to be one of those, Arthur?"

Arthur headed back to his room and began writing more ideas. He quickly scribbled on a piece of paper and was fueled with excitement once again. Minutes passed and Arthur rushed to the kitchen, gleaming with joy.
"Mom! Dad! Look! I know who I want to be when I grow up!" Arthur said.

His mom held the paper right in front of her nose. "Captain of happy people?" asked his mom. Arthur began to steer his imaginary ship wheel and said, "Yes! Everyone who sails with me will be so happy. I'll have games, and stickers, candy and..."

Arthur's mom interrupted -- "Arthur, that's really nice, however I think your teacher wants you to write down a real job. Your Uncle Martin is an engineer. Why don't you write that down?"

Arthur, a little less excited, walked back to his room, sat back in his chair, and stared at the ceiling.

"Engine...neer? ... Is that where I go near engines?" Arthur asked himself quietly. Arthur shook his head in confusion and began writing on his paper. He stared down at his desk and twirled his pencil in the air. His face lightened as he quickly scribbled down another idea.

Arthur walked back into the kitchen at a slower pace, but he smiled as he handed the paper to his mother. Arthur's mother, once more, held the paper in front of her nose while smirking at Arthur's father.

"So you want to be a Master of Playgrounds?" asked his mom.

Arthur replied "Yes! So I'm gonna build everyone their special playground and it's going to be THIS tall and THIS wide and--" Arthur's dad began to laugh out loud. "Oh Arthur, are you pulling our leg? You have to write about real jobs, son. Scientist, accountant, remember your oldest cousin Sarah? She wants to be a dentist!" Arthur touched his wiggly tooth and gave his parents a confused look.

Arthur trudged to his room and slowly closed the door behind him. He slowly rose up to his chair and stared at the blank page before him. With crinkled up ideas surrounding his desk, he picked up his pencil and began to jot something down.

He wedged himself off of his chair and slowly walked towards the kitchen. With tears in his eyes, he slowly gave the paper to his mom and said, "I know who I want to be when I grow up."
Arthur's parents glanced down to see what was written.

Mom and Dad's choice.

"You can pick for me, mom and dad," Arthur said quietly. "I don't think I understand my homework anyways."
With guilty hearts, Arthur's parents stared at each other and began to embrace a sombered and lowly Arthur. "Son, we didn't mean to choose for you. We were just trying to tell you about all the jobs that are out there," explained his dad.

"But my teacher asked me what I want to be when I grow up, she never said what job I want to be. I want to be someone who tells people to have great days, I want to feel awesome, I want to make people happy, and I hope to give them nice gifts. ...And I kinda hope I never have to stop playing outside." Arthur replied.

Arthur's parents bent down to sit next to Arthur.
"Honey, we never thought of it that way. You can be all of those things when you grow up. You can even be those things starting today!" said Arthur's mom.
"In fact, son...I think I want to be those things when I grow up too," Arthur's dad winked.

Arthur ran to his room to grab all the crinkled papers he threw on the ground. Arthur rushed back into the kitchen, holding his papers of wonderful ideas. "Mom! Dad! I know who we can be today!" exclaimed Arthur.

Together, Arthur, his mom, and his dad
then soared, sailed, and dreamed all around the kitchen...

May we all grow up, or grow now...

Arthur becomes a Dad

Arthur's Playground Designs

Principal Arthur

...to be our very own "Awesome Great Day."

To my loving family, especially my Mom, thank you for trusting in me to move thousands of miles away to be my own "Awesome Great Day."
To my husband, John Paolo, may we always encourage our future family to chase every great dream.
- Rachelle

34603799R00019